Little Jay Learns Karate

CREATED BY: GEORGE A. DILLMAN
AND KIMBERLY F. DILLMAN

WRITTEN BY:
CHRIS THOMAS

ILLUSTRATED BY:

DAN ROSANDICH

This book belongs to:

_____

your name

I have read this book ☐ once, ☐ twice, ☐ over and over.

For information about this book write to:
Dillman Karate International, Publishers, 251 Mt. View Rd., Reading, PA 19607 U.S.A.

ISBN: 1-889267-01-5
Library of Congress Catalog Card Number: 96-096949
Copyright 1997
All rights reserved

Printed in the U.S.A.
First printing, 1997

LITTLE JAY EAGLE CAME INTO GRANDPA WALLY EAGLE'S HOUSE CRYING...
TEACH ME TO FIGHT GRANDPA!
WHAT HAPPENED?!

WHEN I CAME HOME CRYING, MY MOTHER, YOUR GREAT GRANDMOTHER SAID SOMETHING TO ME...

SHE BROUGHT ME TO MY GRANDFATHER'S HOUSE, AND MY UNCLE LEON WAS THERE, TOO. THEY ALL BEGAN TO DO A DANCE. WELL, IT LOOKED LIKE A DANCE ME. THEY DID A SET OF MOVES. SOME LOOKED LIKE PUNCHES AN SOME DIDN'T LOOK LIKE ANYTHING I KNEW.

MY GRANDFATHER SHOWED ME HOW TO DO ONE MOVE OF THE KATA. HE HAD ME DO IT OVER AND OVER FOR TWO WEEKS!

THEN WHEN HE THOUGHT I WAS DOING IT RIGHT, HE SHOWED ME A SECRET SPOT ON THE ARM.

BUT, AFTER TWO MORE WEEKS OF PRACTICE, I GOT SO THAT I COULD MAKE UNCLE LEON'S ARM GO NUMB EACH TIME I TRIED THE MOVE

WHENEVER I WOULD MAKE HIS ARM NUMB, GRANDFATHER WOULD TOUCH THE SECRET SPOT AND RUB IT A SPECIAL WAY.

GRANDFATHER WAS PLEASED AND SAID THAT SOON I WOULD BEGIN LEARNING THE NEXT MOVE

ONE DAY AT SCHOOL THE CLASS BULLY GRABBED ME

I WAS ANGRY AND I WANTED TO HURT HIM. SO, I DID THE KATA MOVE AND HIT THE SECRET SPOT ON HIS ARM.

THE BULLY'S ARM DROPPED, AND THEN HE BEGAN TO CRY.
I WAS VERY HAPPY.

I THOUGHT THEY WOULD BE PROUD OF ME TOO, BUT MOM LOOKED SAD, AND UNCLE LEON TURNED AWAY

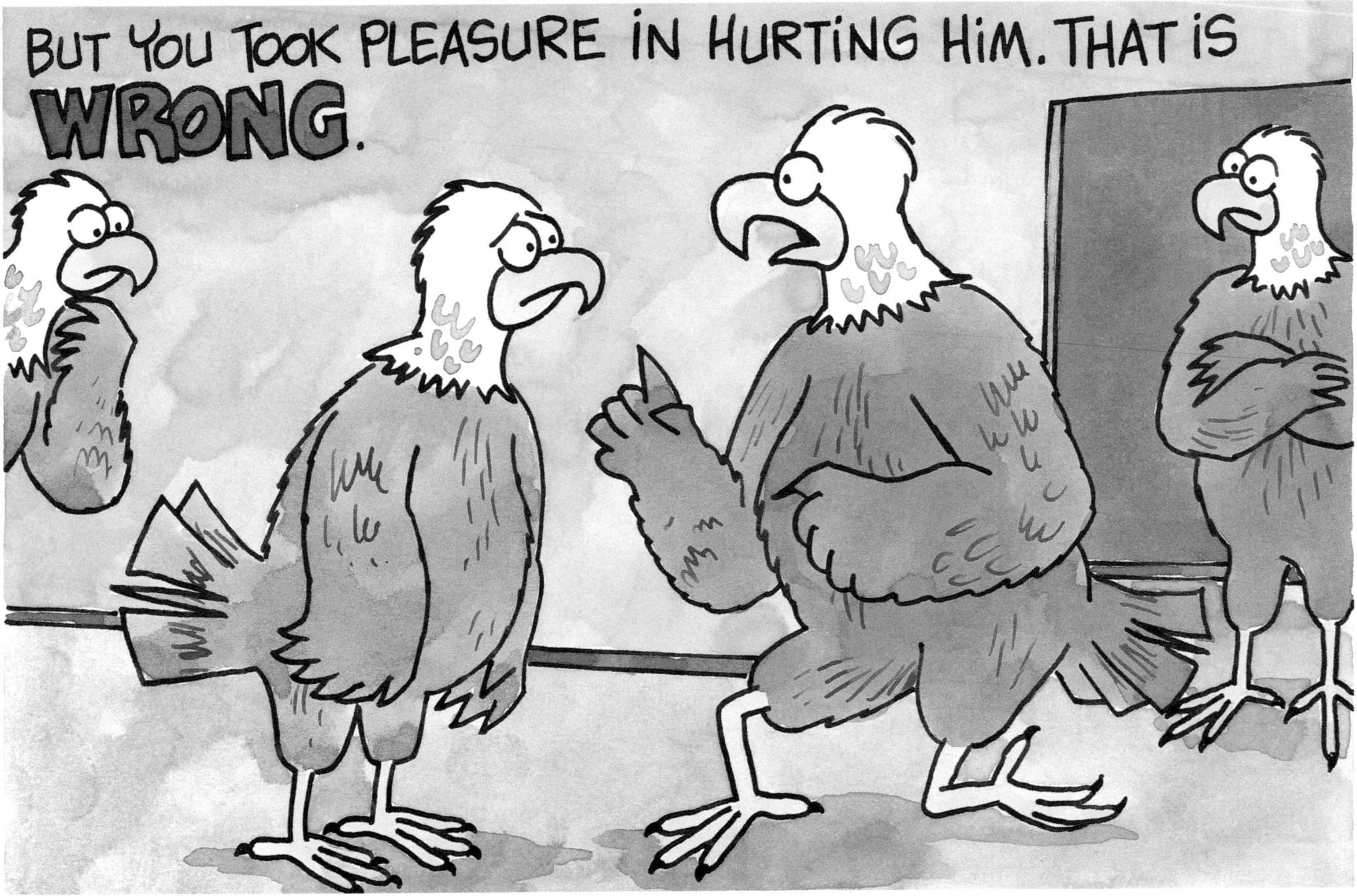
BUT YOU TOOK PLEASURE IN HURTING HIM. THAT IS WRONG.

GRANDFATHER SIGHED DEEPLY

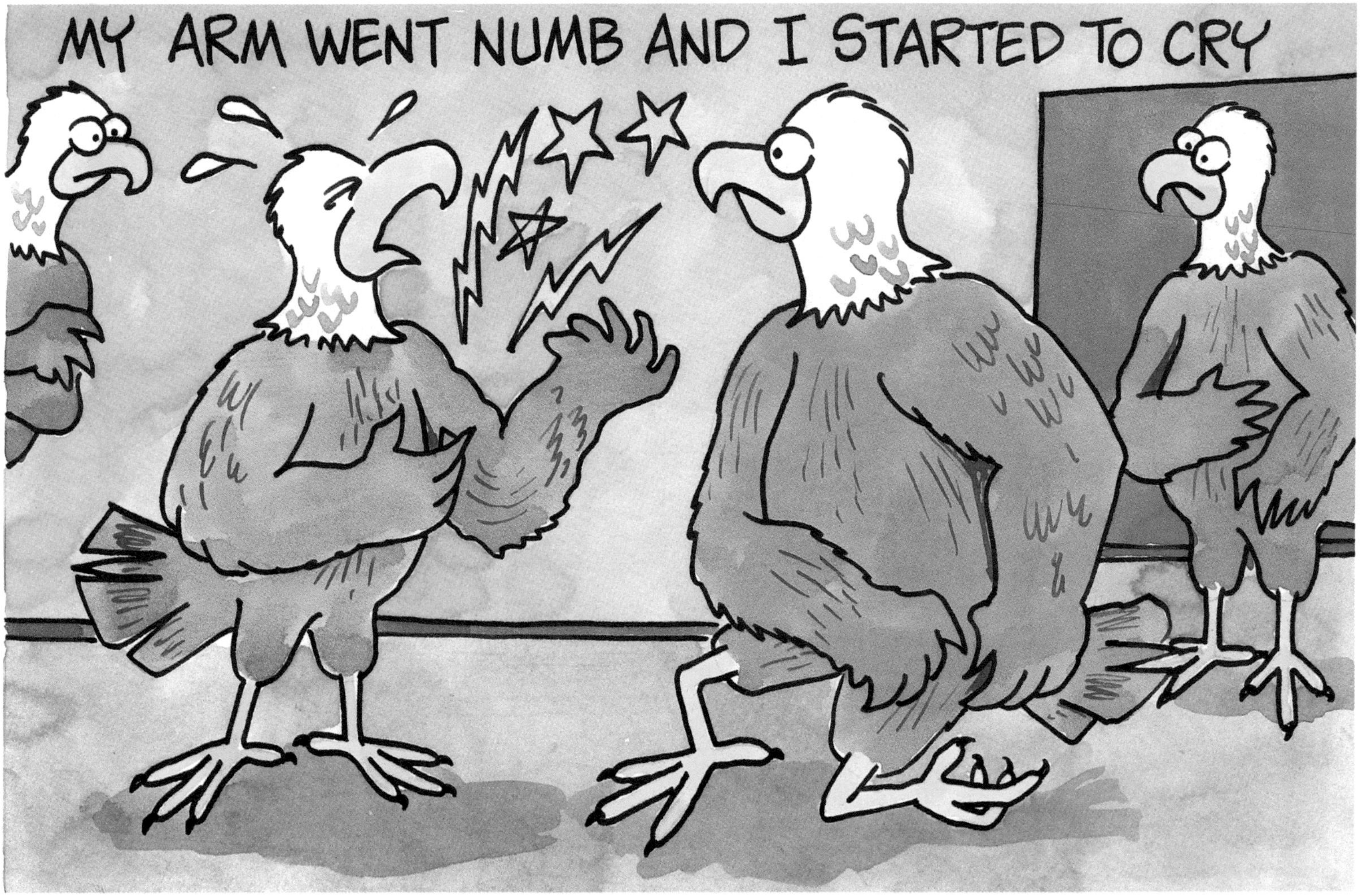
MY ARM WENT NUMB AND I STARTED TO CRY

THEN HE TOUCHED MY ARM AND MADE THE PAIN GO AWAY.

WHEN I THOUGHT ABOUT HOW I MADE THE BULLY HURT AND CRY, I FELT SAD.

Word Game —draw a line from the underlined **phrase on the left** to the box [on the right] that contains the meaning.

1. A <u>bully</u> is...

2. A <u>great-grandmother</u> is...

3. A <u>set</u> is...

4. A <u>kata</u> is...

5. A <u>secret</u> is...

6. To <u>numb</u> is...

7. To <u>pretend</u> is...

8. A <u>hug</u> is...

9. <u>Soaring</u> is...

10. A <u>fighting art</u> is...

flying like an eagle

to stop the feeling in the arm

something only you know

to see the move in your mind

a person who is NOT NICE to others

karate or ju-jitsu

the mother of your grandmother

a group of things

a fighting dance

a way to show you love someone

Reading <u>for</u> **Understanding** — Read the list of questions below. Then, read the story again. See if you can remember the story. If you need to, you may go back to the story to find the answers. When you think you understand the story, discuss your answers with your parents.

1. What happened to Little Jay Eagle ?

2. Who helped Little Jay Eagle ?

3. Who taught Grandpa Wally "the family art" ?

4. What were Great-grandpa and Uncle Leon doing ?

5. What kinds of moves are in a kata ?

6. What happened when Great-grandpa touched the "secret spot" on Uncle Leon's Arm ?

7.   What happened when the class bully picked on Grandpa Wally ?

9. What happened when Grandpa Wally told Great-grandpa what happened to the class bully ?

10.   How did Grandpa Wally correct his mistake ?

For further discussion — Read the list of questions below. Then, read the story again.   Try to put yourself in the place of the characters as they experience the events of the story.   Then, ask your parents to listen to your answers to the questions. Discuss any questions you might have with your parents.

1. Little Jay Eagle asks his Grandfather to teach him to fight. Why does Grandpa Wally tell Little Jay a story instead of teaching him to fight ?

2. How would you characterize the relationship between Little Jay and Grandpa Wally ? (a) respectful, (b) loving, (c) trusting, (d) all of these.   Why ?

3. Why does Great-grandpa have Grandpa Wally repeat the same movement over and over ?

4. What action Great-grandpa performs is meant to teach Grandpa Wally to respect the feelings of others ?

5. Why is Great-grandpa sad when Grandpa Wally tells him what happened to the class bully ?

6. Why is it wrong to feel happy or glad you hurt someone ?

7. Why does Great-grandpa touch the "secret spot" on Grandpa Wally's arm ?

8. What happened when Grandpa Wally told Great-grandpa what happened to the class bully ?

9. What lesson does Little Jay learn from Grandpa Wally's story ? Do you think he is ready to learn karate ?

Chris Thomas, M.Div., is a writer of martial arts articles which have been published in magazines all over the world. Mr. Thomas has also co-authored several books on karate with George A. Dillman. Mr. Thomas holds a black belt master's rank in karate and is a student of both George A. Dillman and Prof. Wally Jay. Chris Thomas lives in Wisconsin with his wife and two children.

Kimberly F. Dillman, M. Ed., is an educator and writer who lives in Reading, PA. Mrs. Dillman also holds a black belt master's rank in karate and is a student of George A. Dillman and Prof. Wally Jay. Mrs. Dillman has written several screenplays, one of which has been made into a feature film. Mrs. Dillman lives in Reading, PA

Dan Rosandich is a cartoonist whose work has been published all over the world. Mr. Rosandich has also designed t-shirts which are distributed around the world. Mr. Rosandich has a large collection of cartoons now available on computer disk which is distributed by The Fun Group, Inc. of Novato, CA. Mr. Rosandich lives in Northern Michigan.

CHRIS THOMAS KIM DILLMAN DAN ROSANDICH

George A. Dillman is a karate expert who is known around the world for his amazing feats.

Mr. Dillman has broken 1,200 pounds of ice and is in "Ripley's Believe It or Not" ® for this performance. He has given demonstrations of karate on television, at live sports events such as baseball and basketball games, and for schools, charities, and other organizations including the Boy and Girl Scouts of America.

Mr. Dillman lives in Reading, PA. From there he travels to other parts of the world to teach karate self-defense to children and adults in all styles of the the martial arts. He is a 9th degree Black Belt, which is one of the highest belts awarded to people who have studied karate for most of their adult lives.

The creative team at Dillman Karate International, Publishing wish to thank Professor Wally Jay of Alameda, CA for his continuing efforts to promote the martial arts.

Without Professor Jay's Small Circle Jujitsu®, our study of karate would not be complete. We are and always will be indebted to him for the knowledge and friendship he has so lavishly shared. We would also like to thank Professor Jay for allowing us to use his family name for the characters in the book.

The first way children learn — even before school—is by role playing behaviors seen and copied in the home. We hope to teach the children reading this book in the same way.

Learn, practice, grow.

ONE MORE VOLUNTEER PLEASE!

DON SPROULE